i

Evincepub Publishing

Parijat Extension, Bilaspur, Chhattisgarh 495001
First Published by Evincepub Publishing 2020
Copyright © Anna Liza Naik 2020
All Rights Reserved.
ISBN: 978-93-90197-24-8
Price: ₹ 158/-

Money Lessons on How to Avoid Daily Financial Stress

Anna Liza Naik

DISCLAIMER

The objective of this book is to render valuable concepts in financial literacy. This book aims to educate and inform readers about personal finance. Book contents serve as a reference and starting guide for anybody who wants to start their journey towards financial freedom. Everybody must gather all relevant information to come up with the right decision to achieve their financial goals. Each person has a different financial situation.

The financial concepts discussed have been verified to the best of the author's knowledge and abilities. However, she cannot guarantee that there are no errors or mistakes. The author disclaims any liability caused by errors or omissions, whether as a result of negligence, accident, or any other cause to any party for loss and damage.

The author has cited examples based on her experience. Therefore, readers need to assess first their current financial situations before applying the strategies the author has shared or without consulting a financial advisor.

DEDICATION

For all people who struggle managing their personal finance,

For all people who want to be financially stress-free,

For all people who want to be financially disciplined and responsible,

This book is for you.

ACKNOWLEDGMENT

This book wouldn't have been possible without the wisdom and guidance of Jesus, my Lord, and Saviour. I give HIM back all the glory and praise!

I'm also immensely grateful to my husband, Harshad who supports me since the day I got the idea of writing this book.

Finally, I want to thank all the people who prayed for me and gave their encouragement as I take this journey of being an author.

May God bless us all!

x

TABLE OF CONTENTS

INTRODUCTION

---◆---

"When should we go to Mumbai?" I asked my husband, Harshad, while we're having lunch near the Pune railway station.

"Maybe around the first week of March? That's a couple of weeks from now. What do you think?" he responded.

"That would be good! Let's visit Mom and Dad before we move to another flat." I positively agreed.

"Uhm, have you heard of this Covid-19?" I inquired of him while we were on the bus heading home. "Do you think it's safe to travel nowadays?" I added.

"Yes, I've heard in the news. But I think there's nothing to worry about it as of now" he replied.

Then everything went fast. Almost two weeks after our Mumbai trip, the government declared a lockdown. I couldn't believe that Covid-19 is now in India! Suddenly, a lot of things have changed. One early morning, I saw a laptop on our table issued by my husband's company for him to start working from home. The society's playground where I used to sit down every evening has become empty and silent.

After several days, I've realized that what's happening is a reality. I have to accept it.

I've observed three categories of people during the lockdown period. First, the front liners and people working in the essentials industry. Second, those people working from home, therefore their active income continued. And lastly, those people who were not earning money. The probationary employees, small business owners, the informal sector, etc. Those who did not earn income during the lockdown suffered from a financial crisis or financial loss.

During these times, I saw the importance of having an emergency fund. In the Philippines, my country, the government declared the first lockdown on 15th March 2020.

After a week, I noticed a lot of people ranting on their Facebook walls about not having money to buy food and necessities. It only means that their money is just enough for daily living. It only showed they did not save for an emergency fund.

The lockdown got extended in the Philippines up to the 15th of May and issues of food and financial support from the government arose.

I believe everybody was affected by this global pandemic financially. By the grace of God, my husband worked from home. His active income continued, so our emergency fund remained intact. However, my equity fund investment was affected because of the economic crash. It was a saddening and frustrating experience to lose some investment but it was incomparable to the fate of people who lost their jobs, businesses, and the people who lost their loved ones due to Covid-19.

I wrote this book "Money Lessons on How to Avoid Daily Financial Stress" to inform people on the proper way of saving, budgeting, building up an emergency fund, and getting out of bad debt. I have included practical tips and activities to do for enjoyable learning. This book serves as a guideline for beginners desiring to learn personal finance. It also serves as a refresher to those people who already have basic personal finance knowledge.

Enjoy reading!

Anna Liza

Anna Liza Naik

CHAPTER 1

THE PROPER WAY OF SAVING

———◆———

Lesson – 1

What is the significance of financial education?

Financial literacy is the effective management of resources and income by understanding basic financial concepts correctly. Everybody needs skill and knowledge to make sound financial decisions on their way to financial freedom. If there are financially educated people, are they financially illiterate? Yes, definitely! Financial knowledge has nothing to do with education. You may have a doctorate, yet mismanage money. You may be at the top of the ladder in your career but careless in managing personal finances. I know a lot who do well in their jobs but with minimal savings. Worse, they are in a pile of debts.

Every day, we face simple or hard financial decisions. Which is cheaper? Packed lunch or dine-in at the office or school canteen? Which is wiser to do? Commute by bus or by cab? Which is better? Credit card or cash? Which is more practical? Purchase a new house or just rent out? If you do not possess the right knowledge in making sound financial decisions, you may experience unfavorable outcomes. The financial issue causes arguments among married couples. Unpaid debts break trust. Friendship breaks due to financial problems. Personal finance is involved in our life's events. Unfortunately, schools never educate us on how to manage personal finance properly.

If you desire to achieve financial freedom, you need the proper knowledge of finances. If you want to be wealthy, you should be financially educated. Learning basic financial concepts is the start of building a solid financial foundation. Financial literacy helps you gain control of your personal finance, end the never-ending debt cycle, understand how money works, and save enough to provide sufficient income for retirement.

———◆———

LESSON - 2

Wrong Money Mindset of People

———◆———

Our current mindset is the total of what we learned from childhood. Our parents or relatives trained us. Our environment influenced us. It is hard to correct the wrong mindset about money and the habits we have developed. Financial education is not just for the affluent, as most people conclude. Financial education is one of the reasons why well-to-do people prosper more. Destitute people and the middle class have the right to become wealthy as well.

A poor mindset thinks that borrowing money is the solution to any financial challenge. Sadly, poor people believe that since they have less money, there is no need to save. Earning a limited income means the more you should save. A lot of people are saving the misguided way without them discerning it. Poor people firstly spend their income and save what is left. However, wealthy people save income and spend whatever is left. The poor and the middle-class worked hard for money, while wealthy people let money work for them. Children at their young age must start learning how to save money. Parents are responsible for teaching them the proper way of saving. The habit of saving is not complicated and easy to learn.

The purpose of this book is to educate people with basic financial concepts. I will discuss the proper way of saving, creating a sound budget, getting out of debt, and building an emergency fund. I will also cite examples of how to apply it daily.

Having financial education is good. However, without applying, it becomes useless. I have written down activities to do at the end of each chapter. I hope that this book will inspire you on your journey to financial freedom.

LESSON – 3

Practice delayed gratification

Most of us want to save money, but we do not believe we can. Isn't it ironic? We desire to own a house, have our dream car, or start up a small business, but everything remains a dream. We want to spend but not to save. People assume that borrowing money is an alternative to saving. It is not the solution to financial challenges. Borrowing money deprives us to save. We have to sacrifice if we want to achieve our goals. Purchasing a house may require sacrificing your travel goals this year. Saving up for business capital may force you to cancel monthly subscriptions of TV cables, cell phone post-paid plans, and others. People must practice delayed gratification by sacrificing the present for a better future.

You must be aware of your spending habits to save money. Think about the future and not just the present. Adjust your lifestyle based on your current income and not vice versa. Buy the things you can afford and not because of wanting. There is no need to upgrade gadgets yearly. Be content in what you have now. You do not need to follow the latest clothing trends. Fashion fads fade quickly. Remember, money not spent is money saved! It doesn't matter how much you earn, even if it's six digits monthly. What matters is your spending habits and ability to save. The bigger the earning, the more chances of saving money!

Saving money takes time. It won't happen overnight. Be patient. It requires a lot of discipline, commitment, and focus. Even if it takes longer, as long as you are heading in the right direction, it's worth waiting. Your reward awaits.

Lesson – 4

The right formula for saving

People are having hard time-saving money because they follow the wrong formula. Let me share with you my mistakes when I was younger. I was following income minus expense equals saving formula (Income - Expense = Saving). I had a lot of expenses which led to no savings at all. I considered all expenses as needs. I had a luxurious life and spent all my income. I prioritized vanity over necessities. This lifestyle made me live from paycheck to paycheck. Yes, no savings at all, literally. Last 2014, I realized I'm getting old and had to start planning for my retirement. It was a wake-up call for me to start saving, budgeting, and clearing out my debts. When I met my now-husband, he taught me how to be disciplined in spending. I learned how not to succumb to impulsive buying. Before spending, I think twice if I am purchasing out of a need and not by my feelings.

If you practice tithing, this is the formula of saving:

Income - (tithe + savings) = expense
100% - (10% + 20%) = 70%
It means you have 70% of your income to spend.

The pay- yourself formula is this:

Income - saving = expense
100% - 20% = 80%
You have 80% of your income to spend.

I will give you a concrete example:

Given: Net income is ₹20,000
Formula: Income (100%) - savings (20%) = expenses (80%)
         ₹20, 000 - ₹4,000 = ₹16,000 left to spend

Here is my tip: Once you receive your income, immediately set aside your 20% savings. Your budget revolves on the remaining 80%. If you do not set aside the 20%, there is a high possibility you'll spend it.

Lesson – 5

Why do we have to save?

1. To build an emergency fund.

Emergencies are unpredictable. Financial preparation spares you from troubles. People get sick and need to see a doctor. Worse needs hospital confinement. You need money for home repairs and fixation of malfunctioning appliances. You have to replace your old refrigerator once it stops working. Do you know the worst thing that may happen? If you lose your job! These are some of the reasons people borrow money since they have no emergency fund.

2. To prepare for retirement through investing.

Retirement is inevitable unless you die young. People who did not plan their retirement rely on government or company pension. Are you sure it is enough? It may serve your daily needs, but what about other financial concerns? Again, borrowing money will be your option. Most people rely on their children or relatives to survive their retirement years. Do not retire as broke because of no preparation.

3. To be a blessing to other people.

It is better to give than to receive as they say. We can share our blessings with other people if we have more than enough. The bible says whoever sows bountifully will also reap the same. God loves a cheerful giver.

4. To have peace of mind.

You cannot buy peace of mind. A night of peaceful sleep is what everybody desires. Can you sleep peacefully knowing that tomorrow is another day of financial problem? These thoughts affect our emotions and decisions. Over-worrying may even lead to anxiety and depression.

Now, we already know that saving money is significant. But how come still a lot of people do not save for their future?

Lesson – 6

Why is it hard to save?

1. Not a priority in life

Many people have a "You only live once" (YOLO) mentality. It is also common in youngsters. A "YOLO" mentality prioritizes the present over the future. Savor each moment and forget tomorrow. It is an alarming habit. How you spend money while young affects your future financial status.

2. No commitment to save.

Commitment keeps you going. It helps you focus on achieving your goal. It drives you to press on when others have already stopped. It motivates you to go on every time you wish to give up. Commitment gives hope in times of hardships. Without it, you will be easily distracted.

3. The wrong money mind-set

A poor mind-set assumes that financial education is just for the wealthy. It believes if a person is destitute hence, no need for saving. Somebody once said to me that the Philippine government takes unnecessary deductions for pension savings. He is ignorant of the fact that he needs income to sustain his retirement days! Pension money will serve as his income if he has one. A poor mind-set only thinks of the present and contented living paycheck to paycheck. There is no financial freedom to such a mind-set.

4. People do not want to sacrifice.

Sacrifice is inevitable if you desire to save and invest. There are things you should learn to say NO to. Say no to frequent shopping of unnecessary household things. Say no to Friday night bar hopping along with friends. There may be a time you have to decline people's invitation to extravagant celebrations. Say no to things and events which require an ample amount of budget. Better sacrifice now, reap your reward later than celebrate now, and suffer in the future.

4. No financial goal

Have you experienced the need of saving money but were not able to do it? I did! I was eager to start for a few months then eventually stopped. Why? I gave in to the temptation of traveling, upgrading my phone, and again succumbed to the new fashion of clothing. How come it happened to me? Because I had no financial goal! I was not committed to the idea of saving. If only I had financial goals, I could have made a down payment to the flat that I want to purchase.

I know someone planned to save for a new car but ended up buying a bike. He purchased the bike out of emotions. Do not buy something out of feelings but always use logic and discernment. Do not be distracted by your surroundings. Be serious in achieving your dreams. Remember, saving money fails without setting a financial goal.

Lesson – 7

How to make a SMART goal?

———•———

(Specific, measurable, attainable, relevant, and time-bounded)

Let me give you a specific example of a short term goal. Please see the breakdown below. I use this strategy in drafting my financial goal, work goal, or even personal goals. You can use this style in any goal setting.

Elements of goal setting are General Objective, Specific Objectives, Strategies, and Tactics.

General Objective: Save ₹24,000 for my online business capital from July to December this year.

Let's analyze the components of the general objective:

Specific goal amount - ₹24, 000
Timeline of saving - July to December this year
Purpose - for online business capital

Set specific objectives to achieve the general objective. Plan strategies to hit specific objectives. Set tactics to achieve strategies.

General Objective: Save ₹24,000 for my online business capital from July to December this year.

Specific Objective:
A. Save ₹4,000 monthly from my income.

Strategy:
1. I will cut unnecessary expenses.

Tactics:
1. Commute by bus instead of a cab.
2. No cool drinks like soda etc. starting July.
3. Carry packed-lunch or tiffin daily.
4. No pay movies from July to December.
5. Reduce dining-out expenses with family by having it monthly instead of weekly.
6. Cancel gym membership. It is better to jog.
7. No out of town travel this year.

You can add up more specific objectives, strategies, and tactics as you wish. Aim to put into action this financial goal. Have focus and discipline. Be mindful not to be distracted. People may laugh and discourage you, just be prepared and ignore them. Now you are ready to draft your own financial goal.

———◆———

Lesson – 8

Activity 1: Setting your financial goal

General Objective:

____

A. Specific Objective:

____

Strategies:
1.____
2.____

Tactics:
1.____
2.____
3.____
4.____
5.____

B. Specific Objective:
1.____

Strategies:
1.____
2.____

Tactics:

1.____

2.____

3.____

4.____

5.____

Drafting a financial goal can be overwhelming. Take your time. Write down all the ideas that you have and then sort out whichever is feasible. Revise your goal if needed.

Lesson – 9

How to save money easily?

Here are the eight ways I suggest:

1. Look for other sources of income

It is easier to save if you have multiple sources of income. However, also be mindful of lifestyle inflation. An increase in income doesn't mean an increase in spending. As much as possible, live below your means.

2. Read financial literacy books and study other sources like video lessons.

Financial education is the key to financial freedom. Your six-digit income is useless without proper knowledge. It's not how much you earn but how much you spend and save. When I was in the Philippines, before coming back to India, I bought several second-hand books on personal finance. I registered myself and attended financial education seminars. My advocacy is that everybody has the right to financial education, regardless of social status. To provide available FREE information in financial literacy, I created my YouTube channel, Anna Liza Naik. I am discussing practical tips in daily financial management. I always believe in practical application and daily use. You can also follow me on my social media accounts Twitter, Instagram, and Facebook.

3. Keep a budget and stick to it.

Track your daily spending by having a budget. List down all your expenses in a notebook, or you may download an expense tracker on your phone. It is easier to reduce expenses if you can monitor your spending. Budgeting money is not easy at the beginning. Don't worry. Surely you'll get used to it.

4. Be content with what you have.

There is no temptation to live a luxurious life if you are content with what you have. Envy is the reason why we compete with other people. Life is not a competition of material things. Do not be jealous of your neighbor's new car. Who knows they may be in debt because of it? Remember, you should know the difference between an asset and a liability. Do not impress people, otherwise, you might end up getting broke.

5. Delaying Gratification

Some people have this "You only live once mind-set". These are the people who live in the present and careless of the future. There is no problem with enjoying the present, but we should also prepare for the future. Getting old is inevitable unless you die young. Who wants to die young anyway?

6. Pay all debts and avoid accumulating new ones.

Clearing all debts is a challenge and takes time. But don't lose heart! Have a goal in mind to be debt-free. How peaceful it is to be free from debts!

7. Stop any form of vices or addiction.

Cigarettes, liquor, and other forms of vices and addictions are stumbling blocks to saving. It is better to save your money instead of spending it on vices. I know someone who sold his house due to gambling. I know a few people who died in sickness because of vices. Addiction won't give you any benefit hence, better stop it.

8. Start saving money as early as possible.

Parents, teach your children at their young age to develop a saving habit. This good habit will impact their future. Time is the greatest ally in investing. Know the importance of compound interest and surely you'll be motivated to invest early.

Lesson – 10

How much do you save when you reduce unnecessary expenses?

———•———

I'm going to give you several examples of potential savings once you cut off unnecessary expenses.

1. Dine- out with family or friends weekly.
   Budget: ₹500 per week
      x 4 weeks

     ————————
     ₹2,000 monthly
      x 12 months

     ————————
     ₹24, 000 in a year

Minimize your dine-out to twice monthly and you will have ₹12,000 savings in a year. That's a huge amount!

2. Traveling or out of town
   Budget: ₹10,000 per travel
      x 3 travels in a year

     ————————
     ₹30,000 total expense in one year

Reduce your travel to once yearly and you'll save up ₹20,000.

3. Vices like cigarette
  Budget: ₹300 per pack weekly
         x 4 weeks

         ————————————
         ₹1,200 monthly
         x 12 months

         ————————————
         ₹14, 400 in a year

Wow! It's really a fortune! Better invest this money. Anyways, we know that cigarette smoking is dangerous to health.

4. Lunch out daily
   Budget: ₹600 per week
          x 4 weeks

          ————————————
          ₹2,400 in a month
          x 12 months

          ————————————
          ₹28, 800 in a year

Carry a packed- lunch or tiffin as much as possible. Food prepared at home is also guaranteed to be clean.

Lesson – 11

Activity 2: Saving insights

Please answer below based on what you have learned in this chapter.

1. What are the reasons why you do not save? Or did not save before?

____

____

____

____

____

____

2. How will you overcome the obstacles of saving money?

____

____

____

____

____

____

3. What are the things you have to sacrifice or let go in order to save more?

____

____

____

____

____

____

____

4. What is your motivation to develop or continue the habit of saving?

____

____

____

____

____

____

____

Lesson – 12

Activity 3: Financial education insights

1. How would financial literacy help you in daily financial decision-making?

____
____
____
____
____
____
____

2. What are you going to do to learn more about financial literacy?

____
____
____
____
____
____

3. How will you explain to other people the significance of financial education?

____
____
____

____

____

____

____

4. What is the most important lesson you've learned in this chapter?

____

____

____

____

____

____

CHAPTER 2

THE STRATEGIES OF BUDGETING

———•———

Lesson – 13

What are the benefits of budgeting?

Have you experienced financial stress in your life? Most of us have experienced it at one point. Have you experienced receiving your income then after a week wondered where it went? What are the common causes of financial stress?

1. People lack emergency funds for unexpected times.
2. Income is not enough to cover monthly expenses.
3. People do not prepare for retirement.
4. Most people are in debt.
5. Sadly, a lot of people live paycheck to paycheck.

Most of us are already aware of these causes. If you are struggling with any of these causes, it's high time to find solutions. One solution to financial stress is proper knowledge in budgeting.

What are the implications of not budgeting? There is a high chance you'll overspend! Without tracking expenses, it will lead to misuse of money.

Discipline is very important for you to have proper spending habits. Spend based on your income capacity. For example, if your income is ₹20,000 monthly, you cannot spend like you are earning ₹30,000. You will surely face financial problems. As much as possible, live below your means. The bible says planning leads to profit, and haste leads to poverty. However, if your monthly income is not enough, you may consider searching for an additional source of income. It will surely help with your budgeting and saving money.

You get financial stress when money controls you. You control your finances with budgeting. It alerts you against possible cash problems in the future. You monitor every cent you spend and cut expenses if needed. More importantly, you set priorities. You discern which items are needs and which are wants.

Lesson – 14

The difference between needs and wants

A need is something that is a must-have in our daily life. It will be hard to live without these items. What are the things we need daily? Food, shelter, clothing, etc. Education and maintenance medicines are also basic needs. On the other hand, wants are the things which give comfort to our daily life and are secondary. We can live properly even without those things. However, wants and needs are subjective. For example, people having online jobs need home Wi-Fi. People living in hot climate countries need air conditioners at home. Filipinos need powdered milk. Fresh milk, since it is expensive in the Philippines becomes a want.

Laundry detergent and shampoo are basic needs. Fabric conditioner and hair conditioner are only add ons. Daily commuting by bus is a need, but frequent commuting by cab is a want. You can wear make-up at work but using expensive brands is your choice. You do not need an expensive watch because a simple one is enough. Realize that local brands can be also of good quality. You do not have to buy expensive ones because you can have good quality products at reasonable prices.

However, nowadays, many people categorize some items as a need because of too much desire to have them. You do not need to upgrade your gadgets because you feel so. You do not need to frequently visit expensive coffee shops just for time pass. You can make a cheaper brewed coffee at home.

Lesson – 15

How do you know if you have proper knowledge of budgeting?

1. You use cash or a debit card instead of a credit card.

It is always better to use cash or a debit card in any transaction. In this way, you can easily monitor your expenditures. You can track which budget category you're overspending.

2. You save first before spending.

Always remember to set aside 20% of your income once you receive it. Set your budget based on the remaining 80%.

3. You prioritize basic needs over luxury.

Prioritizing basic needs requires discipline, especially if you're an impulsive buyer.

4. You monitor daily expenses.

Write down daily expenses in a notebook, or you can download an expense tracker on your phone. In this way, you know where your money is going.

5. You stick to the budget.

Sticking to the budget helps you avoid possible financial stress like debts. Normally, people get into debt when they do not manage their budget well.

———— ♦ ————

Lesson – 16

Spending habits you must stop

———◆———

I was once a money spender. I did not budget money at all! I haven't experienced writing down my daily expenses in the past. I faced financial challenges because of my improper spending habits. Do you have bad spending habits? Check these indicators.

1. You do not get out of the debt cycle

Some people consider debt as part of their lives. They indulge in new debt after paying their current one in full. Keep in mind that borrowing money from people is not the solution to your financial problems. It's a false mind-set.

2. Buying unnecessary items.

Some people love shopping. The idea of shopping excites them. If you have this habit, then better discipline, and control yourself. Prioritize and buy items that are only needed.

3. You are a people-pleaser.

Learn to say no to people, otherwise, it is hard to stick to the budget. When somebody invites you to an event, and you have no budget, be polite to refuse. When someone wants to borrow money from you, and you have no budget, it's okay to say no. Pleasing other people will only get you into debt.

4. You live more than you make.

Nobody gets successful in this bad habit. You won't be able to budget or even save money. Living more than you make is like living in a debt cycle.

5. You lack self-discipline.

Living with self-discipline is not easy but possible. To effectively manage your resources, commit yourself to practice self-discipline in spending. You need an accountability partner like your spouse or friend to encourage and motivate you.

⎯⎯⎯ ◆ ⎯⎯⎯

Lesson – 17

How to budget properly

————◆————

Now that you've come to know the importance of budgeting, let us proceed with the steps on how to do it.

1. List down your expenses.

Write down your expenditures at the end of the day. You can download an expense tracking app or use a notebook. Do not try to memorize your expenses. There is a high chance you will forget the exact amount.

2. Know your spending priorities.

Prioritize necessities over luxuries. You can properly manage your finances in this way.

3. Know how much your net income is.

Be realistic. Set a budget based on your take-home pay. You can allocate your income from your side jobs (if any) to pay your debts or make it as savings.

4. Know your spending limit.

Check your budget first before buying an item. Do you need it now? Or can it wait for the next salary? Do not spend the money that you don't have yet. For example, today is the 12th of the month, and 15th is your salary, do not borrow money today from other people for you to spend and then pay them on the 15th.

5. You can use the budgeting rule of the envelope system, or 50/30/20 rule, or the 80/20 rule.

How to use the envelope system

Household budgeting commonly uses the envelope system. How to use it? You divide the monthly budget into different envelopes, then assign each envelope their corresponding spending category. Do something like this.

1. Label each envelope, for example, household utilities, food, etc.
2. Fill up with allocated funds and also write down the starting amount.
3. As much as possible, spend only what's allocated in each envelope. In case there is a remaining fund, you may use it as debt payment or as savings.

Here is the example checklist:

1. House expenses - electricity, gas cylinder, water bill, home Wi-Fi, house rent or mortgage
2. Food - grocery, meals, dine-out
3. Transportation - car payment, fuel, transportation fees
4. Insurance - health insurance, life protection
5. Debts payment - credit card, personal loan
6. Education - allowance, tuition fee, books, projects
7. Miscellaneous - toiletries, gifts, out of town trips
8. Tithe - 10% of your income
9. Emergency fund - you decide how much you'll allocate monthly

You can add other categories in this example. You can also break it down into details.

A thought to ponder

You are in a shopping mall. You passed by a shirt shop and were tempted to buy a nice shirt. Ask yourself:

1. Is this shirt in my budget?
2. Is this shirt a necessity or a luxury?
3. Should I buy it with cash or credit card?

Let me tell you my personal story. When I was in the Philippines in a shopping centre, I passed by a shoe shop and was enticed to buy a pair of shoes. It wasn't in my budget. I asked myself: Do I need this? Am I going to use it or not? I do not trust my feelings when it comes to shopping since I know I tend to become impulsive. I allowed three weeks to pass before I made a decision. After three weeks, I made up my mind not to buy it since I won't frequently use it.

This strategy requires discipline since most of us have this "I want it now" attitude. But it works!

The 80/20 budgeting rule

The 80/20 budgeting rule sets aside 20% of income as savings and the rest (80%) for expenses. It is just the minimum. You can modify and adjust it to 70/30 or 60/40 as you wish. Sometimes no matter how hard you try reducing expenses, it is still difficult to save. Getting an additional source of income allows you to increase your savings.

The 50/30/20 rule

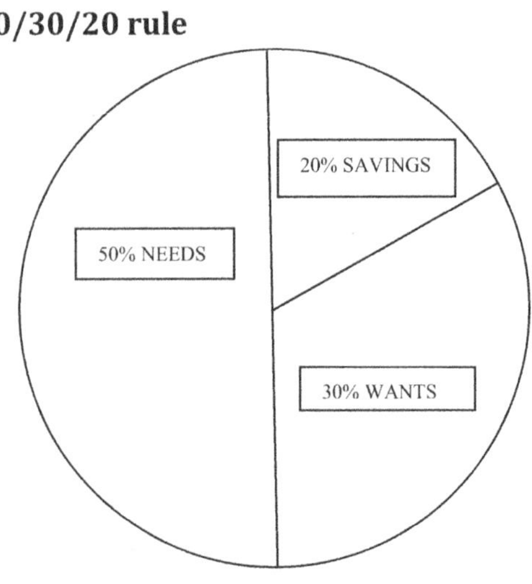

According to this rule, you divide your income to 20% savings, 50% needs, and 30% wants. Once you receive your income, keep aside your savings immediately. Compared to the 80/20 rule, the 50/30/20 rule divides wants and needs. You can include out-of-town trips, eating-out in restaurants, and as many more as wants. People having a high income can easily implement this rule.

I will give you a concrete example. If your income is ₹20,000, the breakdown is:

50% needs - ₹10,000
30% wants - ₹6,000
20% savings - ₹4,000

Lesson - 18

Budgeting myths

I want to share with you the reasons why people are not encouraged to budget their income. These are the three common myths I hear from people:

1. No need to make a budget since income is less.

The more you need to budget your income if it is less! Otherwise, it is hard to manage your income for the whole month. I highly suggest having other sources of income. Even if it gives a small amount of money, something is still better than nothing. I know someone having a minimum salary, yet she budgets well. If she can manage it, you can do it as well.

2. People think that creating a budget is time-consuming.

It will take you some time to adjust and make budgeting as a habit. You don't have to worry! You'll get the hang of it. Don't pressure yourself. Learning a new skill takes time. I have mentioned before that you can either write down your expenses in a notebook or download an expense tracker on your cell phone. Choose whichever is more convenient for you.

3. Some assume that budgeting deprives happiness.

Budgeting serves as a guide and not to deprive you of happiness. Do you know what robs off happiness? Debts, credit, and loans! They give financial stress to people. A financially stress-free life brings peace to everyone. Budgeting is not depriving you happiness. You are just spending your hard-earned money wisely.

Lesson - 19

Activity 4: Create a budget breakdown list

Follow this, breakdown details in creating your budget. Add more categories as you wish.

1. House expenses - electricity, gas cylinder, water bill, home Wi-Fi, house rent or mortgage
2. Food - grocery, meals, dine-out
3. Transportation - car payment, fuel, transportation fees
4. Insurance - health insurance, life protection
5. Debts payment - credit card, personal loan
6. Education - allowance, tuition fee, books, projects
7. Miscellaneous - toiletries, gifts, out of town trips
8. Tithe - 10% of your income (if you believe in tithing)
9. Emergency fund - you decide how much you'll allocate monthly

---

Lesson - 20

Activity 5: Budgeting insights

1. In your current financial situation, how would budgeting help you?

____

____

____

____

____

____

____

____

2. What are the things you thought are needs but now realized are just luxuries?

____

____

____

____

____

____

____

____

____

3. Do you have bad spending habits that need to stop? How will you stop it?

____

____

____

____

____

____

____

____

4. Which budgeting rule are you going to implement? Why?

____

____

____

____

____

____

____

5. Among the three budgeting myths, which one is the most common issue nowadays?

____

____

____

____

____

____

____

____

6. What is the most important lesson you have learned from this chapter about budgeting?

____

____

____

____

____

____

____

____

CHAPTER 3

SAVING FOR AN EMERGENCY FUND

Lesson - 21

Saving for an Emergency Fund

Unexpected things happen whether we like it or not. Hence, we have to prepare. My husband and I moved to an apartment after our wedding. After a few days, we experienced the need of home repairs. Faucet got fixed to fit the automatic washing machine hose. Light bulb got busted easily and other electrical issues. Good thing that there was someone nearby who sorted out everything.

These are unexpected events that require spending. Home repair is inevitable. That's the reason why having an emergency fund is necessary. If we lack emergency funds at that time, either we dip into savings or borrow money from someone.

What are other emergencies that we experience? A sickness that needs a check-up or hospital confinement, your fridge needs replacement, you lost your phone and need to buy a new one, and your laptop got damaged and needs repair. What do you think is the worst? You lose your job! No job means a loss of active income. However, spending continues! You have to buy groceries and pay the bills. The payment of home rental or mortgage still goes on. Payment does not cease. Nowadays, employment doesn't guarantee stability. You should have a back-up plan and an emergency fund serves as a life-saver in these unexpected events.

The general rule for saving an emergency fund is 3-6 months of income. For example, if your monthly salary is ₹20,000, you need ₹60-120,000 amount of emergency fund savings. Sounds hard to save? Relax. Let me continue.

An emergency fund should be liquid and must be accessible in case of need. You can place it in a separate savings account with a debit card or passbook in case you do not want to be tempted to spend money. You can inquire from your bank for any investment that offers a higher interest rate, yet still liquid.

I believe that saving for an emergency fund should be the highest priority of every individual. Without it, your finances can collapse. Having an emergency fund is the first step to get out of debt and to avoid going further into it. Bear in mind that saving for an emergency fund doesn't happen overnight. It takes time.

The idea is to set aside a particular amount monthly until you reach the desired amount needed. You may think 3-6 months of salary is a huge amount to save, but if you commit to saving regularly, then you will accumulate money quickly. Include saving for an emergency fund to your monthly budget. Go back to chapter 2 on budgeting, and you'll see that I included emergency funds in the budget. You can cut back unnecessary expenses or luxuries in case you find it harder to save.

Consider your risk when saving for an emergency fund. The greater your risk, the more you should save. Aim for 6 months of your income instead of 3 months. Consider your employment status. Are you a regular employee or probationary? Is your job category at high demand that even if you lose it, you'll be able to find another job fast? Another factor to consider is your financial status. Do you have other sources of income like a small business, etc.? Or do you solely work in the family? Consider all these to know your risk.

An emergency fund can be short term or long term. Short term can be home repairs and small expenses. Save a short term emergency fund in a platform which is easy to access. Long term emergency fund is for major emergencies like sickness, job loss, etc. Place this fund in a higher interest saving account.

Let me give you an example. Your emergency fund is ₹120,000. Deposit the ₹48,000 in a regular saving account with a debit card or passbook then allocate

₹72,000 in fixed-deposit savings. You can ask your bank for other options.

I want to clarify the events or circumstances which are not emergencies:

1. Getting married is not an emergency.

You have a lot of time to save and plan. Borrowing money from people to spend on the wedding only shows unpreparedness.

2. Save for your holiday or travel plans.

Do not dip into your emergency fund. There is no such thing as an emergency holiday.

3. Giving birth to a baby is not a surprise.

You have nine months to save and prepare for it. Ideally, you should start saving for it once you get married. Sadly, some couples borrow money because of lack of preparation. It's still better to have some cash even if you choose a government hospital over private for giving birth.

4. Purchasing a car or house is not an emergency.

Save 20% of the total amount for the down payment. Taking a loan for the whole car or house amount is unwise.

5. The tuition fee or education fee is also not an emergency.

You have time to prepare and save for the child's education. Education need not be expensive. The success of your child doesn't rely on the institution from where he studied. Send your child to an educational institution that you can afford.

Lesson – 22

Significance of having an emergency fund

Having an emergency fund should be a saving priority for everybody. It is a lifesaver in unexpected events. What are the benefits of having an emergency fund?

1. It prevents you from getting into debt.

You will surely get into debt once you encounter financial problems or dip into your savings. Getting into debt is not the solution to a financial crisis.

2. It helps you protect your budget.

It is easier to stick to the budget if you have a lifesaver fund. Lack of emergency funds may result in mixing up your budget categories.

3. It gives peace of mind.

Emergencies create stress. There is no need to fear if you are ready. Peace of mind is one of the benefits you'll get from having an emergency fund.

4. It protects your investment.

One major emergency can wipe out your investments and savings if you lack an emergency fund. I know a friend who got sick without an emergency fund, therefore, she had no option but to use the fund value of her investment.

It can be overwhelming for people who are new to the idea of building an emergency fund. Do you have a negative mind-set in saving for an emergency fund? Change your mindset before starting to save. Do you believe that saving for an emergency fund should be a priority for everyone? Do you now believe in its importance? Think long-term and think about the future. There may be times when you'll feel discouraged because saving takes a lot of time. Keep in mind the benefits of having a lifesaver fund. Prevention is better than cure. It's wise to prepare now rather than suffer later.

Set saving for an emergency fund to be one of your financial goals. It may take time to achieve your desired amount but be patient. Focus on your goal. Motivate yourself if people try to discourage you. Keep on going and ignore negative people. You'll be distracted if you try pleasing other people. People need self-discipline to achieve their goals.

———— ♦ ————

Lesson – 23

How to save for an emergency fund easily?

Saving for an emergency fund should be part of your monthly budget. I have mentioned it in chapter 2 of this book on budgeting. For example, set a budget of ₹3,000 monthly as an emergency fund. You can automatically transfer it from your salary account to a separate savings account on every payday. You may use the "Keep the Change" strategy. Place any coins or lower bills to a jar or envelope then deposit them in your emergency fund account at the end of every month. You can also reduce expenses by cutting off unnecessary purchases. For example, try carpooling for going to work. I have a friend who tried it, and it works! Try cooking at home instead of eating in restaurants most of the time. I know someone who disconnected her home Wi-Fi since she's frequently not at home. Lastly, I always believe in having an additional source of income. There are lots of opportunities out there! Try part-time online jobs. You can also offer your skills and service during week-offs. You can be an employee yet having an entrepreneurial mindset.

Lesson – 24

Conclusion

Saving for an emergency fund is overlooked mostly by people. It's about time to give it a priority. You'll experience less stress once you save for it. It gives you peace of mind in times of financial distress. An emergency fund protects you from financial troubles. Now is the time to start and save. You can do it!

Lesson – 25

Activity 6: Saving for an emergency fund

1. What is the most important benefit of having an emergency fund?

____

____

____

____

____

____

____

____

____

2. Which platforms do you plan to place your emergency fund? (For example debit account)

____

____

____

____

____

____

____

____

3. How are you going to explain to other people that travel trips, celebrations, etc. are not emergencies?

____

____

____

____

____

____

____

____

4. How does having an emergency fund protect you from financial stress?

____

____

____

____

____

____

____

____

5. What is your plan to hasten building your emergency fund? Write down your detailed plan.

CHAPTER 4

MANAGING DEBTS EFFECTIVELY

Do you know the reasons why you're in debt? Do you want to get out of the debt cycle? Are you willing to change your mindset and behavior towards managing debt?

Managing debt is one of the topics people are not comfortable discussing. Maybe some are avoiding it or considering it as a sensitive topic. Why?

Some people are unaware of the gravity of being in debt. They have this mindset that debt is part of their lives, and it is impossible to get out of the debt cycle. Wrong. People can be debt-free! Yes, it may be hard but possible. Educational attainment has nothing to do with financial literacy. Well-educated people can still fall into the debt trap. I know a successful career person earning a six-digit monthly salary yet taking loans from the bank or people. It has become his lifestyle. Not managing debt properly can become a stumbling block that hinders financial progress. Debt can manipulate people's lives. Now, my question to you is, "What kind of debt do you have? Bad debt or good debt?"

Lesson – 26

Good debt and bad debt

Not all debts are bad. There are so-called good debts. Let's discuss the difference.

Debt is good when you capitalize on it to make a profit. For example, you took a loan to expand your business. Loan serves as additional capital money for business expansion with a hope it will give you profit in return.

I want to discuss more on bad debt since it is a stumbling block to the financial freedom of people. What are some examples of bad debts? Loans to finance a holiday trip, luxuries, and to spend on celebrations. Credit cards not fully paid on its due date fall in the bad debt category. People lacking emergency funds also get into debt. One step to attain financial freedom is to eliminate bad debts.

Lesson – 27

Why do people get trapped in the debt cycle?

———◆———

Some people have the wrong mindset of debt. Here are the few reasons why some people are having a hard time getting out the debt cycle:

1. People claim they need a break or they deserve better.

I agree that working people deserve a break. Holiday travel refreshes body and mind. It makes people feel rested. However, do not get into debt just for the sake of traveling or vacation. Save for it based on your income capacity. Some people think they deserve better like a better phone, a better car, etc. But normally, these so-called better things are not necessities.

2. People are envious of others.

Do you always want to be in fashion? Are you the kind of person who frequently visits expensive coffee shops even if you cannot afford it? Do you envy other people's luxurious lifestyle? Envy can lead to unnecessary purchases. It can lead to living beyond your means, then eventually get into the debt cycle.

3. People desire instant gratification.

These are the people who have a YOLO (You only live once) mentality. They enjoy the present to the fullest and do not care much for the future. People with this mentality tend to be careless with their spending habits, and getting into debt is not an issue for them.

Bear in mind that there is a high chance you will suffer in the future if you cannot make some sacrifices or delay gratification. Unless you die young, you'll surely grow old.

4. Wrong money mindset about debt

Most people think that debt is the solution to financial challenges. Proper budgeting and building an emergency fund is the solution to stay out of debt. It is easier to save than to borrow money. Saving money gives peace while debt gives financial stress. One step to financial freedom is clearing out all bad debts.

———◆———

Lesson – 28

Strategies of getting out of debt

———◆———

1. Debt snowball strategy (or so-called Dave Ramsey's strategy)

The idea in this strategy is to pay off the lowest balance first. Once you start paying off the debt with the lowest balance, you'll be more encouraged and feel a sense of accomplishment. You are more confident and hopeful once one small debt gets paid. There is a mental and emotional satisfaction.

Example:	Interest rate	Amount in Rupees
Loan A	3.5 %	₹20,000
Loan B	6%	₹15,000
Loan C	2%	₹10,000

The loan with the lowest amount is Loan C with ₹10,000, therefore, pay it first. Followed by Loan B, then finally Loan C.

2. Debt avalanche

The idea behind debt avalanche is to pay off the amount with the highest interest rate. This method is the easiest and fastest way of paying a debt. Choose this method if you want to get out of the debt cycle fast.

Example:	Interest rate	Amount in Rupees
Loan A	3.5%	₹20,000
Loan B	6%	₹15,000
Loan C	2%	₹10,000

The loan with the highest interest rate is Loan B with a 6% interest rate, hence pay it first. Followed by Loan A, then Loan B.

Which one is better? It depends on your objective. Choose the debt snowball strategy if you want to be more motivated and encouraged to pay your loan. Otherwise, choose debt avalanche if you like to pay all your debt fast.

Debt is part of the lives of some people. Who agrees with me that a debt-free life is indeed peaceful? You can invest more once you eliminate bad debts and you can spend on relaxing like holidays, and out-of-the-country trips. It's easier to donate to a charitable institution or give gifts to loved ones if you are debt-free. There's a lot of benefits to being debt-free!

Lesson – 29

How to clear bad debt fast?

—————•—————

1. Live below your means.

Don't spend more than you earn. An expenditure higher than income is key to the never-ending debt cycle. You won't be able to save at all. You cannot even start investing. Financial stress will be part of your daily life. How's your spending habit? It has a direct effect on your finances.

2. Don't go into a new debt after the previous one.

Some people consider debt as part of their lives, and that mind-set should be changed. Unless you change your mindset towards debt, you'll live in the debt trap forever.

3. Stick to your budget.

Spend on necessities. If possible, sell everything that you don't need anymore, then allow your profit to pay bad debts. You can have a garage sale or similar to that activity.

4. Add more sources of income.

Having other sources of income will surely help you pay debts. It will increase your savings and the opportunity to invest, too. I believe that it's always better to have another source of income aside from employment.

Lesson – 30

Proper usage of credit card

How would you know if you are a responsible credit cardholder? Firstly, you must be financially capable. There's no point in having a credit card if you are not working or having a business. Meaning, you should have a source of income to pay credit card on or before its due date. Second, you should have financial discipline. Impulsive buyers and people who do not exercise household budgeting will have a hard time managing their credit cards. It is easy to swipe, but it's hard to pay.

What are the advantages of having a credit card?

1. It offers convenience. You don't have to carry a lot of cash. Not carrying much cash is safer especially when you're in a crowd of people.

2. You can enjoy the rewards and cash like travel points or grocery discounts.

3. In case you have a business, paying in credit cards can give you a good credit score.

Lesson – 31

What are the tips in managing credit cards wisely?

————•————

Credit cards are mainly for convenience if there is no cash. It serves as a cash replacement. However, some people have the wrong mindset in using a credit card. It is not for taking loans. Do not use a credit card if you cannot pay in cash. Pay in full the credit card balance before the due date to avoid interest. A credit card is like a temptation for impulsive buyers to overspend. Think before you swipe. Avoid making cash advances. Having a credit card entails financial responsibility to the cardholder. If you think you cannot manage to have a credit card wisely, better not to get one. Otherwise, it can push you into debts.

————•————

Lesson – 32

Activity 7: Managing bad debts

1. Why are people not comfortable discussing debts?

2. How would people change their mindset that bad debt should not be part of their lives?

3. Which do you prefer? Snowball strategy? Or debt avalanche? Why?

____

____

____

____

____

____

____

4. Do you have a credit card? How do you manage it properly? If none, what's the reason for not having one?

____

____

____

____

____

____

____

____

Congratulations! You have finished reading and studying the money lessons to avoid daily financial stress. Now is the time to apply the proper way of saving, budgeting, building up an emergency fund, and eliminating debt. For practical financial tips, you can follow me on Instagram, Facebook, and Twitter. For more money lessons, subscribe to my YouTube channel, Anna Liza Naik.

Please keep watch for the release of my next book!

Made in the USA
Monee, IL
07 July 2026